Dani loved the Labor Day barbecue. She chatted with her aunties, uncles, and cousins who made the drive from Hilo, Hamakua, and Kona. She did notice that Damien's friend and Carmen were missing from the group. She didn't even want to think about what they might be doing.

Joe was across the table from her. Good old Joe. Ever since his family moved to the ranch when she was six, she and Joe had been best friends. "No date?" she asked him.

"Nope. You?"

"Nope. I guess you'll have to be my dance partner."

"Yup," Joe said. "Guess I will."

"Hoo-Wee," yelled Alex, Dani's youngest sister. She stood with her boyfriend, Jackson, at her side. He wrapped his arm around her shoulder. "I have an announcement," Alex said, her mouth all twitchy and eyes opened wide. "Jackson and I are getting married on New Year's Eve!"

Everyone, except Dani, clapped and hooted. She just stared at the happy couple.

"And I hope that my sisters will be my bridesmaids and that everyone here will come to our wedding."

*Cripes,* thought Dani. *Now I will be the last sister to get married.*

Dani's dad gave a toast and then Patti and Marcela both stood at the same time. "You go first," Marcela said.

"Congratulations, Alex and Jackson. I hope you'll be as happy as we are, and I especially hope the bridesmaid's dresses are not going to be fitted, because I'm pregnant!"

"Me, too." Marcela hugged Patti and they both jumped up and down.

Dani reached for another malasada and downed a glass of wine.

# ONLY ON VALENTINE'S DAY

## JACKIE MARILLA

Copyright © 2014 Jackie Marilla

Books to Go Now Publication

All rights reserved.

ISBN-13:978-1495359293

ISBN-10:1495359298

## DEDICATION

A warm mahalo to my husband, a great cheerleader, even without the pompoms.

JACKIE MARILLA

"Hold your horses, Marce," Dani Cabral called through her bedroom door. "I'm almost done."

Dani stood back and admired the completed shadow box filled with her sister's wedding mementos: photographs, lace, dried flowers, and imitation wedding bands. *There's the second one for a sister,* she thought. *My own memory box will have a red valentine with my wedding photo smack in the middle. That is...* Dani sighed. *When I finally get a man to marry me.*

She checked herself in the full-length mirror before she left her room. Marcela was home from Maui with her new husband, Damien, and they promised to bring a friend with them. A single male friend that met Dani's criteria—he was not a cowboy. Dani patted her fuzzy brown hair into place only to have it spring back to its original mayhem. She opened a drawer in her vanity, selected a red, sequined headband and slapped it strategically on her head. The red coordinated with her fingernail polish and the flowers in her calf-length skirt. She dabbed some glittery shine to her full cleavage and wished her hips weren't so ample, but what could she do?

Dani found Marcela sitting on the floor in the hallway when she emerged from her room. "Where are your jeans? This is a barbecue, Dani."

"Did he come? Your friend?" Dani asked.

"Yeah. He's here all right, but you're not gonna' like what you see when you get downstairs."

"Why?"

"The early bird gets the worm, and you took too long. He's already nuzzling up to Carmen."

"Carmen's here? I didn't even know she was invited."

"She rode out with Auntie Nora."

Dani raked her hands through her hair, leaving the headband askew. A low growl emanated from her sternum. She pouted. "It's not fair, Marce. I'm the oldest. I want a husband, and I can't even get a date. At this rate, I'll never reach my deadline."

Marcela stood and reached to fix the mess that was her sister's hair. "Don't worry, Dani, someone will come along. Now, show me the shadow box. I can't wait to see what you came up with."

\*\*\*\*

Joe Domingos stood at the barbecue grill with three of the other ranch hands and Marcela's husband, Damien. Damien was doing most of the talking. When he mentioned the friend they brought with them, Joe's ears perked up.

"Marcela says to me, 'you have any friends on the Big Island, who aren't cowboys?' And I tell her, 'yeah, there's Dirk and Marty.' And she says, 'invite the nicest one to the Labor Day barbecue. Maybe we can help get Dani hooked up.'"

"Is that the dude I saw go in the main house? The one with the city shoes?" Joe asked.

"That's Marty. Chasin' tail early on."

Joe glanced at the Cabral house, laid down the barbecue tongs, and marched across the lawn to the kitchen door. "Need help carryin'?" he asked Mrs. Cabral.

"You're a life-saver, Joe. We'll need all these pots taken to the table, the sweetbread, and Patti's malasadas for dessert. Get some help from the others. Tell my sons-in-law to hop to or they'll have me to answer to." She grinned and tossed a pair of insulated mitts to Joe. He picked up a pot and carried it to the outdoor buffet table and rustled up some help. While Mrs. Cabral tried to organize the men, Joe slipped into the dining room to see if he could find Dani—or, more accurately, if he could tell if she was already hooked up with Marty, the city slickin' tail chaser.

His heart fell to his boots when he saw Marty leaned up against the doorway to the parlor and heard him say in a disgustingly deep voice, "I'll have to scold Damien for waiting so long to introduce us."

Joe hung his head and wondered, again, why Dani was so hell-bent on dating city guys. He wanted to interrupt, but he wouldn't. Dani needed to find her own way.

Just then he heard Marcela squeal from the top of the stairs. "It's perfect. I love it, Dani. I can't wait to show Damien." The two sisters came bounding down the stairs, Marcela hugging a shadow box to her chest.

"Hey, Joe," Dani said.

"Hey, Dani." Joe's heart resumed its rightful position.

\*\*\*\*

Dani's parents took their places at the ends of the makeshift table. As the ranch managers, her parents had hosted many of these events over her lifetime. Her mom welcomed everyone and her dad gave a blessing before they all served themselves from the galvanized silver stew pots and chose their meat fresh off the grill.

Patti, her very domesticated twenty-two year-old sister made fresh Portuguese donuts to die for. At ten, she was able to drop the malasada dough into the sizzling hot oil without burning herself. Even at twenty-four, Dani couldn't get near the stove without some mishap or other—a burn, catching the dishtowels on fire, or drying out the food so much it was unrecognizable.

Dani loved the Labor Day barbecue. She chatted with her aunties, uncles, and cousins who made the drive from Hilo, Hamakua, and Kona. She did notice that Damien's friend and Carmen were missing from the group. She didn't even want to think about what they might be doing.

Joe was across the table from her. Good old Joe. Ever since his family moved to the ranch when she was six, she and Joe had been best friends. "No date?" she asked him.

"Nope. You?"

"Nope. I guess you'll have to be my dance partner."

"Yup," Joe said. "Guess I will."

"Hoo-Wee," yelled Alex, Dani's youngest sister. She stood with her boyfriend, Jackson, at her side. He wrapped his arm around her shoulder. "I have an announcement," Alex said, her mouth all twitchy and eyes opened wide. "Jackson and I are getting married on New Year's Eve!"

Everyone, except Dani, clapped and hooted. She just stared at the happy couple.

"And I hope that my sisters will be my bridesmaids and that everyone here will come to our wedding."

*Cripes,* thought Dani. *Now I will be the last sister to get married.*

Dani's dad gave a toast and then Patti and Marcela both stood at the same time. "You go first," Marcela said.

"Congratulations, Alex and Jackson. I hope you'll be as happy as we are, and I especially hope the bridesmaid's dresses are not going to be fitted, because I'm pregnant!"

"Me, too." Marcela hugged Patti and they both jumped up and down.

Dani reached for another malasada and downed a glass of wine.

****

As soon as the hoopla died down, the table was cleared and the men carried the pots back to the kitchen where Joe found Dani standing over the tray of sugary donuts. As she reached for another fat-laden treat, Joe laid his hand on hers.

"Hey. The music started. How 'bout that dance?"

He lifted the wineglass from her other hand and set it on the counter.

Dani followed him out the door and across the lawn to the plywood dance floor. Joe noticed the city slicker and Carmen finally emerged from wherever and were dancing with arms wrapped around each other and hands in each other's back pockets. Joe had slow danced with plenty of women, but he had never held a woman that tight before. He briefly wondered what would happen if he tried it with Dani. No, she was drunk. And as much as he wanted her, he wouldn't take advantage of her.

Joe took Dani's hand, and they assumed the familiar stance for the two-step. She rested her left hand on his shoulder and extended her right arm outward. He laid his right hand on the small of her back and led her around the dance floor.

Dani's forehead fell forward and landed on Joe's chest. He took a minute to breathe in the coconut scent of her hair before guiding her to a bench on the sidelines.

"I heard Marcela loved the shadow box," he said.

Dani scrunched up her eyes and pursed her lips. "Joseph Domingos, tell me the truth. What's wrong with me?"

Joe answered this question every time Dani was depressed, or drunk, or both. "Nothin's wrong with you, Dani."

And the follow-up question, "But how can my sisters, who are all younger than me, be married or almost married?"

"Because you haven't found the right man yet," Joe said, even though he believed differently. And then, because Joe knew how to make Dani smile, he asked her to describe the wedding of her dreams.

"It's on Valentine's Day. That's important. It's Valentine's Day and everybody is at the Catholic Church in Kona, not the one in Pahala or Na'alehu. Kona. And the priest is standing at the front of the church and anthuriums are all over the place. The red ones. The ones that look like hearts. And my sisters are all dressed in red satin gowns, and the groom and the groomsmen have on red vests and..." Dani held up her fingers to show how long and continued, "little red bowties."

Joe smiled at her and imagined himself dressed in a red vest and red bowtie.

"My dad walks me down the aisle. And I'm wearing a white on white Hawaiian gown with a scoop neckline with poufy ruffles and a built in four foot train that will be hitched up for dancing at the party."

"It sounds beautiful," Joe said.

"It is. And the reception will not be on the ranch. It will be on the lawn of the Kona Breezeway Inn and the cake will be heart shaped with red frosting. Lots of frosting, Joe."

"Just the way you like it."

"Yup."

All of a sudden, Dani leaned forward. "I think I'm gonna' be sick."

\*\*\*\*

Dani shielded her eyes from the sunlight that streamed through her bedroom window. She dragged herself out of bed and walked down the hall to rinse her face with cold water and swallow a couple of aspirin. She knew how bad she looked, but it was Sunday and it was her turn to help with the church's day care. Dani tried to convince herself that children didn't notice things like blemishes on the tip of your nose. *Ugh,* she thought. *How many malasadas did I eat?*

Talk about gluttony. She thought she remembered Joe taking her away from the temptation. She'd have to thank him later.

The thirty-minute car ride to Pahala was nauseating. Her dad teased her no end about 'knowing your own limits,' and her mom talked about the upcoming nuptials for Alex and Jackson. When they arrived at the church, her sisters piled out of Patti's van, and Patti handed over her two-year-old. Kea Boy immediately touched the pimple on the end of Dani's nose and said, "Owie."

The next two hours seemed like an eternity. Dani barely participated in the conversation on the way back home. She took one look at herself and her fat and sugar induced "owie" in her compact mirror, and knew she had to make some drastic changes if she was to ever find a husband.

Dani needed to leave the ranch.

\*\*\*\*

Early Monday morning, Joe and Dani were in the stables saddling their horses to go check the fencing on the northeast section of the paddocks. Joe loved these kinds of days. The pastures were green and the footing on the trail was easy in this section. Much better than along the south end. The sun was shining and not a cloud was in sight. And the best part was that he had Dani to himself for the next seven hours.

Joe hadn't seen Dani at all on Sunday. She usually worked on her shadow boxes after church.

"What'd you do yesterday?" he asked as they headed north along the fence line.

"I made a big decision."

"About a shadow box?"

"No. About my life," she stated.

"What's wrong with your life? Don't let Alex and Jackson's engagement get you down."

"It's not just their engagement. Or the fact that I'm the oldest and don't even have a prospect for a husband. I realized yesterday that nothing will happen for me if I don't take action, so I decided that I'm leaving the ranch and moving into Kona."

Joe stopped his horse. "Kona?"

"I figured it out, Joe. I have 165 days until Valentine's Day of 2015. That's a Saturday. The best day of the week to have a wedding. In 2016, Valentine's Day is on a Sunday, so that is my second choice. I can't find a husband if I don't expand my ability to meet people."

"Okay. Yeah. I see your point. What about your work on the ranch?"

"I haven't told my parents yet, but there's always some young buck looking for work around here."

Joe coaxed his horse forward. He could hear Dani talking behind him.

"Wish me luck."

Joe wanted to be supportive. He wanted Dani to be happy. He wanted to tell her good luck, but instead, he nudged his horse into a full gallop.

\*\*\*\*

On Tuesday, Dani took the day off work to go to Kona. She hopped in her '98 Ford Escapade, rolled down the windows because the air conditioner had long ago quit working, and drove the seventy-five miles to Kona. She parked her car at the Kona Breezeway Inn and filled out an application. The woman who interviewed her was very nice and offered her a temporary, full-time position as a waitress until the regular staff member returned to work. Dani couldn't believe her luck. It was the first job she'd ever applied for, and she got it.

Next, she called her cousin, Carmen, who was looking for a roommate. Carmen welcomed the chance to split the rent, and Dani could move in right away.

That evening at the dinner table, Dani announced that she was moving into town. She told her family about her job and the apartment and asked for their blessing.

"I don't understand," her dad said. "What does Kona have that we don't have on the ranch?"

"Bachelors," Patti said.

Dani blushed.

"Is this true?" her mom asked. "You're going to town to try to meet a man? None of your sisters left the ranch to find a husband."

Dani took a deep breath. "But I don't want to marry a cowboy. I want a city guy."

"Aye. We can't stop you. You're nearly twenty-five years old."

"My point exactly," Dani said.

\*\*\*\*

Dani settled into the one bedroom apartment on Lako Street and started waiting tables that week. She came home to an empty apartment most of the time, as Carmen was either at her job or at Marty's place.

Every day when she got off work, Dani walked along the beach and collected shells, small pieces of coral, driftwood, and sea glass to use in her shadow boxes.

Every night before going to sleep, she called her parents to say good night and then she called Joe. They talked about what they did that day and Joe shared stories from the ranch and Dani shared stories from the Kona Breezeway Inn. Two weeks after she'd arrived in Kona, Dani was able to report to Joe that she had her first date.

"He works at the dive shop across the street. He comes in the restaurant for lunch."

"Hmm. What else do you know about him?"

"Nothing. He works. He's cute. He's available. And he wants to go out with me."

"Where you goin'?"

"To a party at the beach."

"Day or night time?"

"Cripes, Joe. Night time. Why are you asking all these questions?"

"Just making sure you're being safe."

Dani let out one of her little growls. "I'm not ten anymore."

"No, you're not. Which reminds me, are you coming home for your birthday?"

"I hadn't thought about it. I'll have to check my work schedule for next week." *And see how it goes with the new guy*, she thought.

\*\*\*\*

Dani pulled off the highway fifteen miles out of town. The red engine light was on and steam was rolling out from under the hood of her car. "No, no, no," she cried as she dropped her head to the steering wheel. It was her 25th birthday and she didn't want to be alone. She had squelched her earlier aspirations for going out to a fancy dinner with the guy from the surf shop. Joe was right. She should have checked him out.

Dani agreed to drive out to the ranch to spend her birthday with her family. Now that her car was acting up, Dani couldn't get back to the people who actually wanted to spend her birthday with her. Her mom even bought lamb chops because Dani told her she loved them, when in fact she had only tasted them once at the restaurant where she worked. She wasn't really that crazy about them, she thought it sounded impressive to say you loved lamb chops. At any rate, Patti called yesterday to check on the cake preference and Dani cried when Patti said she missed her.

Last night on the phone, Joe said he had a surprise for her. Now she was stuck and alone, and her cheap go phone was dead because she forgot to plug in the charger.

She blew her nose, wiped her eyes with the back of her hand, and cursed the brown goo clinging to her thumb. The no-run mascara was a joke. A few little tears and away it went streaming down her face with a mind of its own. Dani gathered up her purse and worthless phone and stepped out of her broken-down car and hitchhiked for the first time.

Luckily, the first person who stopped was an older woman who repeatedly said, "oh, my," every time Dani told her something. She was nice enough to drive Dani all the way to her apartment and then handed her two dollars as a birthday gift. Dani thanked the woman, called her an angel, and then let herself into the lonely, hot apartment. She found the power cord for her phone and plugged it in, waited twenty minutes, and then called home.

"What? Who is this?" Patti asked.

"Dani. It's Dani."

"Dani. What's wrong?"

"My car broke down. I got a ride back to the apartment, but I'm stuck. I can't come home."

"I'm sorry. I'll talk to Dad and see what we can do. Talk to you in a few minutes."

The click of the phone made Dani cry all over again. She finally washed her face, put on her pajamas, and opened the refrigerator. Her choices were slim. She could have peanut butter or ramen noodles. She wanted birthday cake. And lamb chops. And her family.

The ring of her phone startled her.

"Dad is sending Joe with a tool kit and tow bar to get your car off the road. He'll be there in a couple of hours."

"Patti?"

"Yeah, Dani?"

"Would you send some cake with Joe?"

\*\*\*\*

Joe loaded up the truck and headed out. He would still get to Dani's before eight and they could eat her birthday supper together after he towed her car.

Joe banged on Dani's door just after eight. "Happy Birthday."

Dani threw her arms around Joe. "Thanks for coming. I see you got my decrepit car towed off the road."

Joe blushed. Dani usually only touched him when she was drinking or they were dancing. It felt good to have her so close. "Yeah, I'll look under the hood in the morning. Now, we need to call your family and let them know what's up."

After Joe assured Dani's dad that the car was safely off the road and Dani's family sang Happy Birthday to her, Joe hung up the phone and went back out to the truck to get a box. "Birthday party in a box," he announced.

"Food." Dani was practically salivating.

Mrs. Cabral sent lamb chops, mashed potatoes, string beans, and coleslaw. Patti sent the whole cake and a box of candles.

Joe and Dani sat side by side on the Formica countertop. They laughed and ate. Joe thought the only thing that might make it better was if they were dancing so he could feel Dani's body next to his.

Joe got in the food box, found the candles, and counted out twenty-five. He put them all on the cake and sang to her in a silly, twangy, country voice.

She clapped and blew out the candles.

"What'd you wish for?" Joe asked.

"Wouldn't you like to know?" She giggled and Joe's pulse quickened.

"I brought champagne and beer," he said.

"Ooh. Champagne. Definitely champagne."

Joe opened the bottle and looked around for glasses while Dani licked the icing from the candles.

"We only have coffee mugs," she said.

"Then that's what we'll use," Joe replied. They toasted to her birthday and ate cake.

"Two pieces max," Dani said as Joe served the cake. But they left the cake sitting on the counter between them as they perched on the countertop, and Dani continued to eat forkfuls of cake until only half remained.

Joe asked about the surf shop guy and she made a disgusted face. "It was awful. I'll need another drink to get through the whole story."

Joe poured her another mug of champagne and opened a beer for himself.

Dani started, "So I met him at the beach for the party. Marcela told me not to tell new guys where I live until I know them really well, so I drove myself." She took a big gulp of champagne and dipped her fork into the chocolate icing and scooped a mouthful. "At first, he seemed all gentlemanly. He introduced me around and kept one arm on my shoulder, real protective-like."

Joe looked at his boots and sucked in his breath.

"Anyway, just when I think this might be a guy I could fall in love with, he does the crudest thing! He drops his shorts and takes a leak, right in front of me and everybody else, and then waves his thingy around. It was disgusting."

Joe couldn't control the grin that crept over his face.

Dani punched him in the arm. "What? You think that's funny? Even on the ranch, you guys are more discreet than that!"

"That's because we're cowboys. And cowboys are gentlemen."

Dani raised her glass. "I'll drink to that."

Joe hopped off the counter and told Dani he'd be right back. He went out to his truck and got her presents. Dani's eyes opened wide when she saw the five carefully wrapped packages.

"For me?"

"One at a time, in order. Patti made me promise. First, from your parents." Joe handed her an envelope. When Dani removed the card, a check fell to the floor. "That will be a check for twenty-five dollars. Mom and Dad always give us checks. One dollar for every year we've been alive. I can really use it this year to buy some food."

The gifts from her sisters were all supplies for her shadow boxes. Patti and Kea bought her a machine that cuts paper into fancy designs. Marcela and Damien gave her a stack of fancy paper and ribbons, and Alex and Jackson got her three rolls of lace.

Joe handed her a little package from her two-year-old nephew, Kea Boy. It was a bottle of acne cream for her "owie." Dani touched her nose and laughed. "I'll probably need that after all the cake."

There was one more gift on the counter. "Who's that from?" Dani asked.

"Open it," Joe said as he handed her the box covered in shiny red paper.

Dani carefully removed the paper and folded it up. She looked at the box, then at Joe. "Is it really?" Joe handed her his pocketknife and she slit the tape on the edges. Tears streamed down her face as she peered inside the box.

"Try it," Joe prompted.

Dani took the digital camera from the box, and Joe handed her a battery from his pocket. She snapped a picture of Joe and then looked at the image and burst into fresh tears. "How could you afford it?"

"I don't need much, Dani. The ranch gives me most of what I need, so I've been saving for awhile."

"Oh, Joe, thank you. It's perfect." She leaned over and gave him a peck on the cheek.

He felt the heat rise up in his body and a yearning to feel those lips again. He turned to face her, but she was examining her new camera. That one kiss would have to last him.

Joe jumped off the counter and leaned over to pick up the check that had fallen from the card from Dani's parents. "You should look at this," Joe said.

Dani took the check from his hands, looked at the check, and did a double-take. "$250.00?"

"I was talking to Patti about your shadow boxes and how you like to put pictures in them. So she talked to your parents and they wanted to give you enough money to take a photography class at the community college." Joe pulled a flyer from the college out of his back pocket. "Classes start in January."

"Wow. They've never given me such a big gift before."

"Patti thinks you could take pictures to earn some money. You know, graduation pictures, weddings, birthdays. Some of these people in Kona actually pay someone to take pictures of their babies every three months!"

"Really?"

"Patti also thinks you could sell your shadow boxes with people's pictures in there."

Dani just shook her head. "Do you think I can do it, Joe?"

"I think you can do whatever you want."

Dani slid off the countertop and held the camera at that height. She carefully set it down and pushed some buttons. "Hurry, Joe. I set the timer. Scrunch in."

Later, when they looked at their picture on the camera, Joe thought, *Could be lookin' at a married couple.*

****

Thanksgiving Day at the ranch was always a noisy occasion. Country western songs blared from the CD player with the whole family singing along, pots and pans clanked in the kitchen, and the screen door banged as the other ranch families joined the festivities. Mixed aromas floated gently on the breeze: turkey and sage, pumpkin and cloves, marshmallows and sweet potatoes. Dani stood in the middle of the kitchen enjoying every last bit of it.

She hadn't been eating very well since her position at the restaurant ended and she was starved for home cooked food. Patti slapped her hand when she reached for a taste of the turkey, just out of the oven. Dani laughed and reached a second time, just to see her sister's reaction.

Dani raced up the stairs and got her camera from her overnight bag. All of a sudden, she yearned to have photos of everything and everybody from the ranch. She took photos all day as if she could capture the essence of the ranch and take it back to Kona with her when she left in the morning. Dani tried to convince herself that the tug in her heart to move back to the ranch was due to her fatigue. She tried to reason with herself that she would not find a husband by staying at the ranch and that Kona was her home now. She was a city girl, darn it, and if she didn't work her master plan, she would have no chance of finding a husband, never mind having a Valentine's Day wedding! As it was, she only had eighty days to Valentine's Day.

Dani waved to the cowboys coming in from morning chores. They all tipped their hats. She remembered what Joe told her. Cowboys are gentlemen. She shook her head in approval and went to her bedroom to freshen her make-up and change into her skirt.

A bang on the door and Marcela blew in and hugged her tightly. Dani could see the little bulge starting to show. She patted her sister's tummy. "How's it going?"

"The doc says it's all good. And I feel great. I found these jeans, see?" She lifted up her long-tailed shirt and there was a stretchy band around her middle and her jeans were unzipped about half way.

"Just can't let go of those jeans, huh?"

"Just can't let go of those skirts, huh?" Marcela answered.

Dani explained, "If I looked as good as you do in tight jeans, I'd wear them more. But with hips like mine, a skirt is more flattering."

"You look like a Cabral woman in your jeans. Like a real cowgirl."

"Just what I wanted to hear."

****

That evening, Dani sat on the lanai in the porch swing looking at the photos she had taken: the cowboys riding in from morning chores, Patti in the kitchen with her mom, Marcela and Patti's baby bumps, the pastures with the wind-blown ironwood trees, and her extended family gathered around the Thanksgiving table.

Joe appeared and produced a bottle of red wine and two glasses. "Want company?"

"I thought you were a beer drinker?"

"I am with the cowboys, but I sort of like sharin' a bottle with you when I can."

"Joe, when was the last time you had a date?" she asked him.

"I don't know. High school prom, maybe. Does it count if it was your cousin?" he chuckled.

"Who was it again? The one from O'ahu with the freckles?"

Joe nodded.

"I remember she wore a black dress and a dog collar with spikes on it."

"That's the one," Joe said. "Mom thought I should go to the prom, and I couldn't come up with a date, so she and my auntie dreamed up a solution."

"You weren't the only one who went with a cousin. Remember who I went with?"

"That's right." Joe slapped his knees and laughed uncontrollably. "Carmen's brother. What a nerd. He barely paid attention to you, he was so busy on his cell phone."

"He couldn't even do the two-step."

They sat in silence for a few minutes. "You didn't exactly answer my question, Joe. Why aren't you dating? You're not…you know…not interested in girls?"

"Damn it all. Why would you think that?"

"Because you're two years older than me and the only cowboy on the ranch who's not married or engaged."

Joe took a deep breath. "I'm just waiting for the right one."

"Me, too."

"When do you have to go back to town?"

"Early in the morning. My new manager at Wal-Mart gave me today off only if I promised to do a double shift tomorrow."

"Do you like it? Your job?"

Dani thought about that. She liked earning money so that she could afford to stay in Kona, but she really yearned to do something more creative. "It's okay, I guess. Helps pay the bills."

"Let me know if ya' need anything."

"I will."

On Sunday when Dani called to check in with Joe, she reported that she simply had to pay more attention to her timeline. "I can practically hear the clock ticking," she told him. "You know it's only—"

Joe finished her sentence. "Seventy-six days."

"How do you know that?" she asked.

"It's mostly what you talk about, Dani."

"Well, it's important, you know?"

"I know. Talk to ya' tomorrow."

"Yeah. Good night."

Just then Carmen and Marty came bounding in the door with a man that could only be described as heaven-sent. He stood a full foot taller than Dani and his eyes matched the colour of the ocean fronting Kailua Bay.

"Meet Derek, Marty's older, single brother," Carmen gushed. "We're goin' to Mauna Kea to watch the sunset and stare at the stars through the telescopes. Wanna' go?"

Dani bobbed her head up and down. "Yeah, I'll go. Let me get some jeans on."

She changed into a pair of jeans in the bathroom and then found a long sweatshirt that covered her hips. *Cripes,* she thought. *I get a chance with a guy and I have to wear jeans to keep warm.*

She joined the others in the living room and Derek immediately took her hand to walk out to the car.

Her feet barely moved as she floated toward her destiny.

\*\*\*\*

The next night, Dani called her parents to say good night and then called Joe. "Guess what I did last night after we talked?"

Joe said, "Went to bed early?"

"No. I went to Mauna Kea with Carmen and Marty and Marty's brother."

Joe didn't say anything.

"It was like a date. He held my hand and opened the door for me." Dani took a breath. "He's a banker, Joe. An honest-to-goodness city guy."

"Where's he stayin'?" Joe asked.

"At Marty's."

"For how long?"

"I don't know. Long enough to have another date on Saturday night. You should be happy for me. This is only the second time someone asked me out since I moved to town."

"Sure, Dani. I'm happy for you." He did want her to be happy. He just hoped that she would be happy with him. He hated to admit it, but he hoped Marty's cousin turned out to be as disgusting to Dani as the surf shop guy—maybe more.

****

On Christmas Eve, Dani arrived at the ranch with her entourage just in time for the evening meal. It was one of the times when the family celebrated privately in the main house at the dining room table. The only other family members who regularly joined them were Auntie Nora and Carmen, but when Dani realized that Marty and Derek had no other family to spend Christmas with, she insisted they come out to the ranch. Besides, Dani couldn't wait to show off Derek to her sisters.

When Dani introduced Derek to her family, she could tell that her sisters thought he was handsome. Marcela gave her a thumbs-up when Derek wasn't looking. Dani's mom called everyone to the table.

After Derek's hands were free from passing around the serving dishes, Dani felt his hand on her knee. A smile as wide as the north pasture crept over her face and stayed there the entire meal.

Everyone lingered for what seemed like hours. Alex and Jackson shared their wedding plans, Marcela and Patti talked about their pregnancies, and Dani's folks kept making side-glances at the banker from Kona. Finally, Carlota stood up and announced that she had laid out clean bedding for Marty and Derek in cabin three, Auntie Nora could sleep in the guest room, and Carmen could share Dani's bedroom. It was an invitation to leave the table and get ready for bed.

Dani walked Derek down to the cabin while Carmen and Marty stayed at the house to visit a while longer with Carmen's mom. She showed him the idiosyncrasies of the cabin. "If it gets too cold, here are some spare blankets. The hot water only works for the tub, not the shower, and if you hear sounds in the night, it's likely the cats racing around on the metal roof."

Derek pulled her to him and clutched her ample hips. Their lips met and he started to caress her in ways he hadn't before. "You are driving me crazy, baby."

She kissed him deeply, hungry for his compliments.

He moved his hands down her thighs and started to lift her skirt. She pushed him back a little and giggled. "Not here, Derek."

"Where?" he asked. "When?"

"Later. We'll talk about it later."

She kissed him one final time. "See you in the morning for church. I'll be the one wearing red," she teased.

The next morning when she woke up, she noticed the twin bed assigned to Carmen had not been slept in. Maybe she stayed in her mom's room, Dani thought, as she got ready for church.

Dani especially loved Christmas morning Mass, and the feeling of hope that emanated from that service. And this year she would have a man at her side, just like her sisters. And her parents would quit making side-glances at Derek once they saw he was willing to attend Catholic Mass.

She walked down to the cabin and knocked on the door.

A groggy Marty answered in his boxer shorts, grumbling, "What the hell? What time is it?"

"Merry Christmas to you, too. It's time to get ready for church."

"We're not going."

Dani nodded. "Would you please wake Derek up so he can go to church with us?"

Derek appeared in the doorway of the bedroom, rubbing his eyes. "Hi, baby. What's up?"

She crossed the room and gave Derek a kiss. "Merry Christmas. It's almost time to leave for church."

"Mmm," he grabbed her backside and pulled her to him. "Not today, baby. I'll just stay here and keep

Marty and Carmen company. Want to skip out with us?"

"No," she said. "I thought you were planning to come to church."

"I'm not really a church kind of guy."

Even his goodbye kiss didn't fix the hurt that swelled up in her. Now she would have to explain why her new boyfriend was skipping out on church on Christmas. He wouldn't earn any brownie points with her parents.

As she slid into the car, she mumbled something about Derek not being able to join them because the cats kept him up all night.

Dani thought about Derek during the whole service. She hoped he wasn't serious about not being a church guy, because she wasn't sure she could marry someone who wouldn't attend church with her family. At the end of the Mass, the congregation stood on the front lawn and formed a circle around the crèche to sing

"Joy to the World." Her mom took her left hand, and Joe slipped his hand into her right.

Dani told her parents she'd catch a ride back to the ranch with Joe. She needed a friend to talk to and Joe fit the bill.

"Where's your friend?" Joe asked when they got into the truck.

"At the ranch. He says he's not a churchgoing kind of guy."

"What'd your parents think of him?"

"I'm not sure, but my sisters think he's gorgeous. And he likes me and I like him. He might be the one."

"Hmm," Joe said.

The rest of the day, Dani stayed as close to Derek as she could. After the mid-day meal, Derek asked her to take a walk, and she readily obliged.

They ended up walking to a grove of koa trees. Derek leaned her up against the koa trunk and kissed her until she was breathless.

"Still mad at me?" he asked.

"A little," she admitted. "I want my parents to like you, and going to church would have sealed the deal."

He dove in for a deeper kiss. "I promise I'll go next time, okay?"

Dani needed to believe him. "Okay."

"And then you'll owe me one," he added.

****

Dani looked forward to bringing Derek back to the ranch for Alex and Jackson's wedding. Maybe her parents would get a better impression of him. It was New Year's Eve morning and Derek had slept on the couch at her apartment because Marty and Carmen asked for some private time over at his place.

She leaned over and kissed Derek's cheek. "Morning, handsome," she cooed.

"You know you're killing me, don't you?" Derek droned.

"I told you I don't have casual sex."

"But, we've been dating for over three weeks. Carmen didn't make Marty wait that long. Within an hour, the way I heard it. What's with you? Are you frigid or something?"

Dani straightened up and glared at him. "I just need to make sure you're serious about us before I crawl into bed with you. I've been clear that I'm only interested in a committed relationship. Do you want the same thing?"

He reached for her hands, pulled her on top of him, and kissed her deeply. "You know I'm committed to you, Dani. If I wasn't, I would have been out of here long ago." His arms stayed wrapped around her torso, his hands gently massaging her backside through the fabric of her pajama bottoms. He whispered that he had never known anyone as beautiful as she was and that he wanted her in the worst way.

Dani held his gaze, and then boldly initiated a kiss, her hands against his bare chest. Derek moved his hands to the elastic on her pajama bottoms and slid his hands under them to cup her backside. She moaned as he cradled her curves, and then gasped as he slipped his hands into her panties. She could feel his erection and tried to wriggle off him.

Derek moaned and shook his head, pulled her back on top of him and kissed her eyes, the tip of her nose, then her ear. "I want you. Come on, Dani."

"I can't," she said as she moved off him.

"God, Dani. I love you. Is that what you want to hear?"

She answered in a small voice. "Only if you mean it."

He sat up and headed for the bedroom. "I love you, Dani, and if you come to the bedroom, I'll prove it."

She followed him to the doorway. "You know I can't right now. I'm already late getting out to the ranch to help with the wedding." She wrapped her arms around her man and kissed him. "I love you, Derek, and I want the first time to be special. Don't you?"

"I guess. But give me something. Tell me when you think you'll be ready."

"I'll tell you after you say it again," she coaxed.

"I want you, Dani." Derek moaned.

"I know that. Say you love me and when we get back from the ranch, I promise I'll sleep with you."

"I love you, Dani."

\*\*\*\*

Dani was giddy the whole two hour drive out to the ranch. Derek, Marty, and Carmen would drive out later for the wedding. She couldn't wait to tell her sisters and Joe that she thought a proposal was just around the corner. She was sure Derek was the one. He'd said that morning that he loved her. Every time she thought about those three words, her heart jumped around in her chest. She could have stayed in Derek's arms all day listening to his promises of love.

She wondered what it would be like to be married to a banker, what kind of house they would have and who their friends would be. She pictured herself giving parties and hiring caterers. Their children would have their father's blue eyes, not her brown ones. She wondered how many children Derek wanted. She was thinking four, like her own family.

And then, she pictured the wedding. It wasn't too late to have a Valentine's Day wedding. She had a full forty-five days and she knew every detail already. Patti and her mom would help sew the dresses, and Derek made enough money to pay for a catered reception. She pulled off Highway 11 and phoned the Kona Breezeway Inn to see if they were booked yet.

*Oh well,* she thought as she pulled back onto the highway, *Derek can probably afford to upgrade to the Hilton for our reception. They have lots of rooms where we could have it.*

She honked the horn when she pulled into the drive. Her mom waved from the kitchen window. As soon as she entered the house, all her sisters took turns hugging her, then Patti commented that she looked like the one getting married and why was she all of a sudden so darned happy-go-lucky?

Dani jumped up and down and told her sisters that Derek confessed to loving her and that she thought a proposal was just around the corner, maybe even tonight! Dani said her Valentine's Day wedding was just a matter of inviting the guests.

The day was a flurry of activity to get ready for the wedding. Dani followed Alex around with her camera and took candid shots of Alex getting her nails painted by Marcela and her hair styled by Patti. Dani put the camera down just long enough to apply Alex's make-up, and then it was time for the sisters to put on their wedding clothes.

Dani, Patti and Marcela all wore light blue denim dresses, red cowgirl hats, and red boots. Each dress was a little different to accommodate Marcela and Patti's bulging bellies. *Maybe next year at this time, I'll have a baby bump*, Dani thought.

The wedding ceremony lasted only about ten minutes, and then Dani took some photos of Alex and Jackson, and Joe filled in to take photos of the whole wedding party. With that done, Dani walked down to the reception area and found Derek. She sidled up to him and slipped her hand in his. She wanted everyone to know this was her man. She finally had a man!

He leaned over to kiss her square on the mouth and she encouraged his open show of affection. Carmen and Marty wrapped their arms around the two of them, making a sandwich, and telling them to get a room. Dani whispered to Derek, "When we get home, we'll make love all night long." She initiated a luxurious kiss and led him to the dance floor.

It was a slow dance and Derek held her tightly and ran both his hands up and down her back and whispered in her ear that he couldn't wait and wouldn't she change her mind?

She tried to placate him by promising the wait would be worth it. "Now be a good boy while I go take photos of Alex and Jackson cutting the cake."

After the cake was served, Carmen pulled her aside and asked Dani to join her and the brothers for a foursome. "I've had my eyes on Derek ever since he arrived, and I really think you should share with your cousin." Carmen pouted and stumbled against Dani's shoulder.

"You're drunk, Carmen. You don't mean it."

"Yes, I do. It was Derek's idea."

Dani didn't believe her. Carmen was always stirring up trouble, and she seemed insatiable when it came to sex.

And then, Dani saw Carmen lead Derek to the dance floor. His hands grabbed her backside, and she planted her hands firmly on his. Dani wouldn't stand for this! Even if they were drunk, she would not share Derek with her racy cousin. She walked to the dance floor and interrupted their dance.

She smiled at Derek and put her arms around his neck. He put his hands on the small of her back and pulled her to him and gave her a long, slow, kiss. A kiss to knock your boots off.

"We were wondering…" he started.

"Who are 'we'?"

"Marty and Carmen and me. We were wondering if you want to have a little fun."

Dani's stomach turned. "What kind of fun?"

"You know, fun in the sack. The four of us, together."

"You guys are all drunk. Carmen just asked me the same thing." She stepped back from him and led him to a bench away from the dance floor. She thought it best to distract him for now. She didn't even want to discuss the notion of the four of them in bed together.

"You promised," he said.

"Derek, it's New Year's Eve, and we're at my sister's wedding. I did promise you this morning that I would sleep with you. And I will, as soon as we get back to Kona." She leaned in to kiss him and he started to slip his hand up her skirt. She pushed it away.

"Don't be so naughty. It's only one more day."

"But I want you tonight. And if I can't have you, I'll just have to go looking somewhere else."

"You wouldn't do that, would you? If you really love me, then you won't even think about that." Dani pleaded with him.

Derek snickered. "Love?"

"You said you loved me and we were in a committed relationship."

Derek kissed her. "Honey, didn't your mother ever tell you not to believe a guy in heat?"

She slapped his face, and then started to get up. Derek grabbed her and pulled her onto his lap. "Oh, baby, I was just joking. I do love you. And I really want you tonight."

"Shut up," she said and covered her mouth over his. "I'll slip out after the party is over and come to your cabin."

"That's more like it."

"But no Marty or Carmen." She kissed him again. "I love you, Derek, but don't think you can share me with your brother." Dani scootched off his lap. "Wanna' try to dance some more?"

"Nope. You know what I want."

Just then, Dani heard her mom call her name. "Excuse me, Derek. My mom needs me for something."

****

Joe stayed clear of Dani all night. He was in charge of the music, so he couldn't very well leave. He knew Derek was coming, but he had no idea that to see Dani with him would make him so miserable. Every time they kissed, Joe felt sick to his stomach. When he overheard the sisters talking about an imminent proposal, he knew he had to take action or lose Dani forever.

What he'd just witnessed was obviously a disagreement. He didn't like the way Derek grabbed at

Dani and tried to slip his hands up her skirt at a family function. Joe didn't know how Dani could stand him. She kept talking about marrying a gentleman, but this guy certainly didn't match that description. He was as slimy as an eel.

Mrs. Cabral was organizing the father-daughter dance. Joe could see her scurrying around trying to get Alex and Mr. Cabral on the dance floor, and get Dani ready with her camera. In the meantime, slimeball Derek had cornered Carmen and was rubbing up against her like a bull in heat. Joe scoffed. What kind of guy does that to his brother's girlfriend?

Joe had to do something to get Dani away from Derek, even if it meant making her angry. He fantasized all kinds of things in his head. His first thought was to take him out to the pasture and just shoot him. Illegal. Next he thought about strapping Derek to a bull and watching him get bucked to death. Still, illegal. *Snap out of it,* Joe told himself. *You won't kill anybody for real. What else would work?*

Then Joe had a great idea. He would tell Derek that Mr. Cabral wanted him off the ranch and away from his daughter. Not illegal, but a lie. Joe didn't lie. Maybe he'd just go find him after the father-daughter dance and tell him himself what he thought of him. Man-to-man.

Mrs. Cabral gave the signal to shut off the music so she could announce the father-daughter dance. She stood at the microphone with Alex on her right and Adolfo on her left. "This is the third time my husband's had the honor of dancing with one of our daughters at her wedding. And this is the third time you will see me cry. Thank goodness there is only one daughter left to get married!"

Joe put on "I Loved Her First," the song Mr. Cabral insisted was the dance song. Joe imagined Dani dancing with her dad to that song while he stood on the sidelines and cried with Mrs. Cabral. He had to get rid of Derek before it was too late.

After the dance, Dani walked up to Joe and asked if he would keep an eye on her camera. "I need to find Derek. Have you seen him?"

Joe froze. Should he tell Dani that he saw him with his hands all over Carmen? Then he realized what that would sound like, so he said, "Before the dance, he was over there." Not a lie.

"Thanks, Joe."

"Wait, Dani. I need to talk to you."

"Can it wait? I need to work something out with Derek."

"Sure." He had waited for years to say what he itched to say. It could wait a little longer.

****

It was eleven forty-five and Dani wanted to make sure she was with her man when the clock struck midnight. It would be the first time that she had a man to kiss to bring in the New Year. Her year. The year of her Valentine's Day wedding, or at least engagement. Maybe Derek's plan was to get engaged on Valentine's

Day. That would be romantic. She didn't know if she could wait forty-five days, but she felt confident that Derek loved her—he'd said so that morning. And this talk about Marty and them together, well, that was just the alcohol talking. She wondered briefly if she should talk to Carmen about leaving them alone in the cabin. Even at her age, she couldn't disrespect her parents by sleeping with Derek openly, but she could sure tiptoe to the cabin and back to her room without a soul knowing.

She just had to assure Derek that she would come to the cabin. She looked around for Carmen to firm up her plan, but she was nowhere in sight either.

Dani headed down the walkway to the cabin. When she stood at the doorway, she could hear sounds from inside. *Good, he must be here,* she thought, *and it's still before midnight.*

She knocked softly on the door. She heard scuffling and laughter. She knocked again, this time louder. Marty threw open the door with no clothes on.

He reached for Dani's hand. "Oh, baby. You decided to come after all."

Dani shook her head. "I didn't mean to interrupt you and Carmen. I'm just looking for Derek."

He led her to the bedroom doorway. Among the stacks of quilts she could make out arms and legs. Then the quilts parted and she gasped.

"Come on in, baby," a naked Derek swooned, as he cupped Carmen's breast. "There's room for everybody."

Dani ran up the hill to the house where she would spend the stroke of midnight alone—again.

Dani could hear the early morning sounds of people stirring—her dad's distinctive footsteps down the hallway, the whinnying of horses, sounds of plywood being dropped into the pile to be reused for the next celebration at the ranch. Ranch life resumed as if nothing had happened. Didn't they know her heart had been broken, her dream of a Valentine's wedding crushed? Dani dropped her face into her hands. She couldn't leave her room yet. She never wanted to see Derek again. And she wasn't ready to face her family and admit defeat, again. The soft knock on her door and the sound of Marcela's voice made her tears flow harder.

Marcela opened her arms to Dani as soon as the door was ajar. "I heard. I'm so sorry," Marcela patted her sister's back.

"It was awful."

"Damien came into our room this morning with smoke bellowing out of his ears. He went down to the cabin to ask Marty for his car keys because his car was in the way, and when there was no answer, he went on in and looked for the keys. When he saw the three of them in bed together, all hell broke loose and he kicked their asses off the ranch. He's gone, Dani."

"He said he loved me. I thought we would get married."

"Good riddance. Let slutty Carmen have them both."

That made Dani laugh, then cry, then laugh again. She pulled at her hair. "What is wrong with me? Why can't I find a man?"

"Maybe you're trying too hard. It's better to wait for a good man, than to hurry a relationship along with any old sleaze that comes along."

"He didn't seem like a sleaze."

"Well, Damien and I are so sorry for ever introducing Marty to this family. We feel responsible for this whole mess."

"It's not your fault. The worst of it is that I'll spend another Valentine's Day alone. No boyfriend. No engagement. And definitely, no wedding."

"Get yourself dressed. Mom's working on your favorite breakfast and the trail ride starts about ten."

Dani growled a little release growl. "I forgot about the trail ride. Who all knows?"

Marcela scrunched up her nose. "Everybody. Damien was screaming all manner of insults to the threesome. You must be deaf. You might be the only one in a twenty mile radius that didn't hear him."

"How's Auntie Nora?"

"You know her. She came into the kitchen after the uproar and told Mom she was sorry for her daughter's part in the situation, and wouldn't it be nice if you could smack some sense into grown children?"

"What did Mom say?"

"You know Mom. She shook her head and told her sister she knew the feeling."

Dani told herself she should hold her head up high. Everyone on the ranch loved her and they would blame Derek. She might be viewed as the victim. Ugh. That might be worse. Still, her mom had a traditional New Year's Day planned, and the trail ride might be just what she needed to clear her head and figure out her next move.

She would take photos as they went to help take her mind off Derek. She recorded the rolling green pastures, the mix of decrepit wooden fence posts and shiny galvanized metal replacements, the picnic feast, the color of her dad's neckerchief, the flowers adorning her mom's cowgirl hat, her nephew riding in the saddle with his dad, Alex and Jackson on their first day together as a married couple, the smooth curve of Patti and Marcela's bellies, she and her sisters in their red cowboy boots and tight blue jeans, and Joe.

Dani gravitated toward Joe as soon as they headed back to the ranch.

"Hey," he said.

"Hey."

"You okay?"

"Back to square one with a bruised heart to show for it."

"He wasn't the one."

"Nope. He wasn't."

They rode along in silence. Dani stopped occasionally to get off her pinto and take some photos.

"You know I thought he'd propose?" Dani broke the silence.

"I heard."

"I was so sure Derek would ask me to marry him. I even called the Kona Breezeway Inn to see if they were booked for Valentine's Day."

"You did?"

"They were booked. I should have known. It was like a sign, Joe."

They dismounted and took a break under the shade of an old ironwood tree.

"Dani," Joe began, "what do you really want?"

"A husband, kids--at least four—a home with a craft room, maybe a little garden and a dog. Chickens. And a heart-shaped bath tub, as long as we're dreaming."

Dani looked at Joe. "How about you?"

"A wife, kids—at least four—a home with a little garden and a dog." Joe took her hand in his. "And a heart-shaped bath tub."

Dani looked into Joe's eyes. Joe, her best friend and confidant. Joe, who was always there when she needed him. Joe, who wanted exactly what she wanted.

She leaned over and brushed her lips against his.

He pulled her to a standing position and then knelt back down on one knee. "I've wanted to say this since I was eight years old. Dani Cabral, I love you more with each passing day. And if you'll have me, I'll cherish you for the rest of my life."

Dani knelt facing Joe. Tears streamed down her face as she realized that this man, this cowboy, was the one.

Joe reached in his pocket and pulled out a diamond ring with garnets embedded on the band. "Dani, will you marry me?"

She wrapped her arms around Joe and cried and laughed and said yes.

Joe pulled four papers from his pocket and handed them to her. The first two were from the Catholic Church in Kona and the second two from the

Kona Breezeway Inn. One set of papers reserved February 14, 2015 for both places and the other for February 14, 2016. Dani looked puzzled.

"I made the reservations hoping that we would be the couple using them, but it was gonna' be my gift to you if you chose some other guy."

Dani touched his cheek and kissed him more deeply this time. Joe pulled her to him and said, "I've waited this long, Dani, you choose which year you want."

"We have forty-four days to get ready, Joseph Domingos. Are you ready?"

"More than ready, Dani Cabral." He slipped the ring on her finger and tipped his hat.

JACKIE MARILLA

ONLY ON VALENTINE'S DAY

# MEET THE AUTHOR

# JACKIE MARILLA

Jackie Marilla lives on a farm in Hawai'i with her supportive husband, a Rottweiler, several feral cats, and a flock of hodgepodge chickens. She writes contemporary romance set on the Big Island.

When she's not at her desk writing, Jackie loves to visit her grown children and grandson in the Northwest, read, sew, and make lamp work glass beads. In a past life, she was an elementary school teacher.

Jackie is a member of the Romance Writers of America and the Greater Seattle chapter.

# ONLY ON VALENTINE'S DAY